KU-268-033

MAUDE

The Not-So-Noticeable Shrimpton

lauren child

lauren child

illustrated by

trisha krauss

PUFFIN

For Ferdi, Wardi,
Tess and Hector,
with love,
Trisha

For the most
noticeable Delfina,
with love,
Lauren

PUFFIN BOOKS
Published by the Penguin Group: London, New York,
Australia, Canada, India, Ireland, New Zealand and South Africa
Penguin Books Ltd, Registered Offices: 80 Strand, London WC2R 0RL, England

puffinbooks.com

First published 2012

001 – 10 9 8 7 6 5 4 3 2 1

Text copyright © Lauren Child, 2012
Illustrations copyright © Trisha Krauss, 2012
All rights reserved
The moral right of the author and illustrator has been asserted
Made and printed in China
ISBN: 978-0-141-34277-1

The SHRIMPTON family!

Wherever the Shrimptons went people **noticed** them.
They were **so talented**, **so eccentric**, **so larger** than life . . .
you just **couldn't miss them** even if you wanted to.

The Shrimptons hated to be missed.

They spent a great deal of time and trouble making sure that they never went unnoticed.

Mrs Shrimpton created *flamboyant* hats from feathers, fruit and fur. Her latest had a live peacock positioned perkily on top.

Mrs Shrimpton's hats were real head-turners.

Mr Shrimpton had a moustache
so **long** and so *twirly*
butterflies liked to
perch on it.

It was quite a statement as moustaches went.

Penelope Shrimpton was *dreadfully* beautiful.

She could **STOP** traffic just by walking out of the house. She caused frightful street jams.

People *gasped* when they saw her turn the corner.

Hector Shrimpton was a mesmerizing mover –
toe-tappingly mesmerizing.
He wore his tap shoes in maths class,
at tap class and everywhere
in between.

$$4\frac{2}{3} + 7\frac{1}{9} = 4 + \frac{2}{3} + 7 + 9$$

$$= 11 + \frac{2}{3} + \frac{1}{9}$$

$$= \frac{99}{9} + \frac{6}{9} + \frac{1}{9}$$

$$= \frac{106}{9}$$

**It was
heel toe,
heel toe
wherever he went.**

Constance Shrimpton had
a voice like *music*.
An '**um**' or an '**ah**' from her could get

all the birds in the trees atwitter.

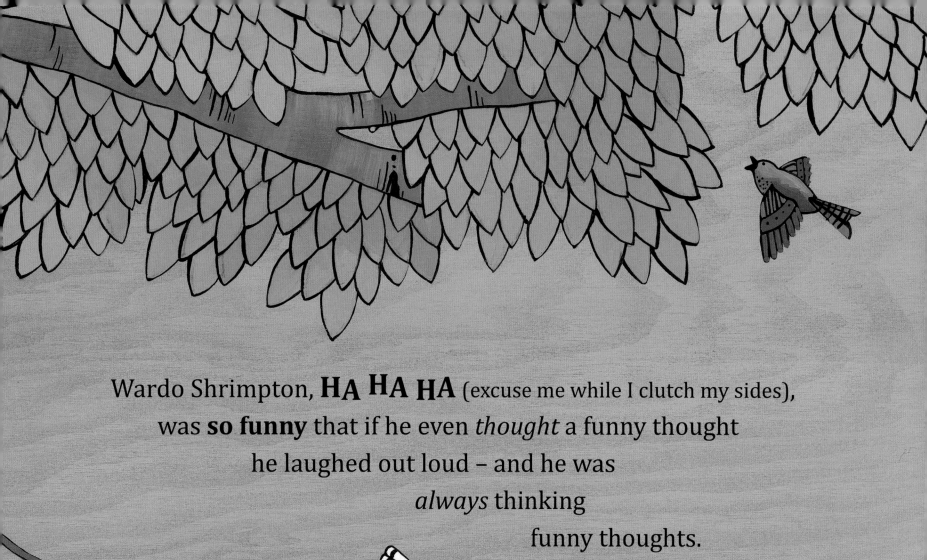

Wardo Shrimpton, **HA HA HA** (excuse me while I clutch my sides), was **so funny** that if he even *thought* a funny thought he laughed out loud – and he was *always* thinking funny thoughts.

He was a **laugh a minute** and no one found him **funnier** than he did.

Being **noticed** was what all the Shrimptons lived for.

All except, that is, for Maude Shrimpton.

Unlike Penelope,
when Maude crossed the road she had to **dodge** cars.

She moved so
inconspicuously
that when she
performed in her
school play
people thought she
was part of the scenery.

Her voice was so small that not even the Shrimptons' collection of unusual dogs could hear her.

And **dogs**, as you know, have *exceptional* hearing.

No matter what she wore
Maude just seemed to *merge*, to fade, to disappear.

She was what you might call a *blender*.

People often remarked, "What a shame it is for the Shrimptons that their middle child isn't more . . . **something**. She doesn't seem to have a talent for *anything* and it is so **important** to be good at, well, at least one thing. **She's just so bland.**"

All in all Maude Shrimpton
stuck out like a very sore thumb.

**Well, she would have if you had
actually ever noticed she was there.**

Now one day Mrs Shrimpton said,
"Maude, it will soon be your **birthday**.
What would you like as a *present*?"

"Something *startling*?"
swooned Penelope.

"Something
striking?"
stammered Hector.

"Something
stupendous?" sang
Constance.

"Something **silly**?" sniggered Wardo.

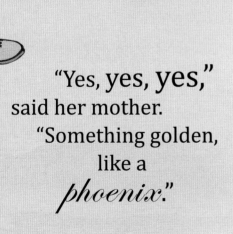

"A goldfish," said Maude.

"What a *marvellous* idea,"
exclaimed her father.
"A **GIANT** carp or a **whale!**
Something enormous."

"I want a goldfish," said Maude.

"Yes, yes, yes,"
said her mother.
"Something golden,
like a
phoenix."

"Just a goldfish,"
said Maude.

So on her birthday
Maude Shrimpton,
with great excitement,
unwrapped her
present.

Maude found it quite *embarrassing* to step out
of the house
with a TIGER
in tow.

Everyone **looked.**

But all the other Shrimptons simply *loved* how people **stared**

as they strolled along the boulevard with a **GIANT CAT**.

The tiger could do wonderful tricks.
My, was he eye-catching.

Those **daring** leaps,

those **impossible** feats.

Such **stripy** stripes,

such **long sharp** claws,

such **pointy** teeth, such a **BIG** appetite . . .

And that's the thing to
remember about tigers:
they do get **very** hungry.

And when a tiger is hungry . . .

it is VERY hungry indeed.

And so it was that one Tuesday in August Mrs Shrimpton returned from the shops to hear a terrible ROAR!

"Whatever's that about?" she said.

"We have run out of tiger food," said Maude.

"RUN!" shrieked Mrs Shrimpton, holding on to her panicking peacock hat.

YUM, thought the tiger.

"Hide!" shouted Mr Shrimpton, his moustache all aquiver.

"Quiet!" gasped Constance, setting all the birds atweet.

"Tip-toe," stuttered Hector, tip-tapping his shiny shoes.

And Maude just stood completely still.
Can YOU see her?

Sometimes, just sometimes, *not* being noticeable is the very best talent of all.